When we perform the story though, Annie the acrobat really does walk on her hands, just like she does in the book. My great-niece is very good at gymnastics, so she sometimes plays Annie. I ask members of the audience to play the other circus characters, and my husband Malcolm plays Sam Sly.

Of course the book wouldn't be complete without Lydia's wonderful illustrations, which I really love. Actually, Lydia knew that Malcolm would play Sam Sly on stage, and I think she drew him to look a bit like my husband. But Malcolm is much nicer than Sam!

And now Sam Sly, the Singing Mermaid, Annie the acrobat and all of her friends are 10 years old, and I would like wish them a very happy birthday.

Julia Donaldson

THE SINGING MERMAID

For Eilidh and Mhairi ~ J.D.

For Amelia and Imogen ~ L.M.

First published 2012 by Macmillan Children's Books
This edition published 2022 by Macmillan Children's Books
an imprint of Pan Macmillan
The Smithson, 6 Briset Street, London EC1M 5NR
EU representative: Macmillan Publishers Ireland Ltd, 1st Floor,
The Liffey Trust Centre, 117–126 Sheriff Street Upper,
Dublin 1, D01 YC43
Associated companies throughout the world.
www.panmacmillan.com

ISBN: 978-1-5290-6928-0

1 3 5 7 9 8 6 4 2

A CIP catalogue record for this book
is available from the British Library.

Printed in China.

THE SINGING MERMAID

JULIA DONALDSON ★ LYDIA MONKS

MACMILLAN CHILDREN'S BOOKS

Did you ever go to Silversands
On a sunny summer's day?
Then perhaps you saw the mermaid
Who sang in the deep blue bay.

She sang to the fish in the ocean,
To the haddock, the hake and the ling,
And they flashed their scales and swished their tails
To hear the mermaid sing.

And sometimes the singing mermaid
Swam to the silvery shore.
She sat and combed her golden hair
And then she sang some more.

She sang to the cockles and mussels.
She sang to the birds on the wing.
And the seashells clapped and the seagulls flapped
To hear the mermaid sing.

When Sam Sly's circus came to town,
Sam took a stroll by the sea.
He heard the mermaid singing
And he rubbed his hands with glee.

He said, "I can make you famous."
"I can make you rich," he said.
"You shall swim in a pool of marble
And sleep on a fine feather bed.

You shall sing for the lords and the ladies.
You shall sing for the Queen and the King,
And young and old will pay good gold
To hear the mermaid sing."

"Don't go! Don't go!" cried the seagulls,
And the seashells warned, "He lies."
But the mermaid listened to old Sam Sly
And smiled as she waved her goodbyes.

And he took her away to the circus,
And she sang to the crowds round the ring,
And "More! More! More!" came the deafening roar
When they heard the mermaid sing.

And she made good friends with the jugglers
And the man who swallowed fire,
And the clown with the tumbledown trousers,
And the woman who walked on wire.

But she wasn't friends with old Sam Sly.
No, she didn't care for him,
For he made her live in a fish tank
Where there wasn't room to swim.

And there was no pool of marble.
There was no feather bed.
And when she begged him, "Set me free!"
He laughed and shook his head.

All summer long the circus toured,

All autumn,

winter,

spring,

And many a crowd cheered long and loud
to hear the mermaid sing.

But the mermaid dreamed of Silversands
And she longed for the deep blue sea,
And her songs grew sad, and again she said,
"I beg you, set me free."

But again he laughed and shook his head.
And he told her, "No such thing.
Here you will stay, while people pay
To hear the mermaid sing."

At Silversands, a seagull
Was flying to his nest
When on the breeze he heard a song,
The song which he loved the best.

And he followed the song to the caravan.
Sam Sly was about to lock it.
The seagull watched as he turned the key
And slipped it inside his pocket.

The seagull waited till Sam had gone.
Then he perched on the windowsill.
And tap-tap-tap at the window
He tapped with his yellow bill.

"Come back! Come back to Silversands.
It's only a mile away.
I can find the key and set you free
If you'll come back home to the bay."

"Escape!" barked the dogs. "Escape!" miaowed the cat,
But the mermaid sighed: "I'd fail,
For how could I walk to Silversands
When I only have a tail?"

"Like this!" cried Annie the acrobat,
And she stood upon her hands.
"This is the way, the only way,
To get to Silversands."

"Right hand, left hand, tail up high,
There's really nothing to it.
If I give you lessons every night
You'll soon learn how to do it."

Next week, while Sam was snoring,
The seagull stole the key.
He carried it off to the caravan
And set the mermaid free.

And he flew ahead, to guide her,
As she walked upon her hands,
All along the moonlit road
That led to Silversands.

And the creatures on the seashore
And the fish beneath the foam
Jumped and splashed and danced with joy
To have their mermaid home.

And she sang to the cockles and mussels.
She sang to the birds on the wing.
And the seashells clapped and the seagulls flapped
To hear the mermaid sing.

And if you go down to Silversands
And swim in the bay of blue
Perhaps you'll see the mermaid,
And perhaps she'll sing for you.

I was very excited when Julia wrote *The Singing Mermaid*, so I got started right away, as always, with some paintings of the main characters to work out how they should look. Here are some early versions of the mermaid and the wicked circus owner, Sam Sly. Sam started out with very black hair, but then I decided to make him a little greyer. I tried a few different shapes for his nose too. Can you spot the one I chose to go with in the end? The mermaid didn't change too much, but her tail and her hair were a different colour when I first painted her. What colour would you paint a mermaid's tail?

Once I know what the characters will look like, I draw very small, sketched versions of each page. These little versions are called 'thumbnails' and they help me to work out how I would like to illustrate each moment of the story, and what I'd like to show. I also start thinking about what colours I would like to use at this stage too. This saves lots of time later on!